THE PROMISE PROBLEM

By Christy Webster

Based on the episode "A Thomas Promise" by **Rick Suvalle**

A Random House PICTUREBACK® Book

Random House New York

CREATED BY BRITT ALLCROFT

Based on the Railway Series by The Reverend W Awdry.
© 2022 Gullane (Thomas) Limited.
Thomas the Tank Engine & Friends™ and Thomas & Friends™ are trademarks of Gullane (Thomas) Limited. © 2022 HIT Entertainment Limited.
HIT and the HIT logo are trademarks of HIT Entertainment Limited.
ISBN 978-0-593-43162-7 (trade)
rhcbooks.com
www.thomasandfriends.com
Printed in the United States of America
10 9 8 7 6 5 4 3 2 1

It was a beautiful day on the Island of Sodor. Thomas the Tank Engine was playing Stack the Tracks with Carly, a crane car. His best friend Percy watched, and the fix-it engine, Sandy, cheered him on.

Thomas knew he could do it. He was the number one engine.

He kept the tall stack steady as Carly reached way, way up . . . and placed the final track!

"Ta-da!" Thomas peeped.

"We knew you could do it!" Percy said.

"*Toooooooot!*"

Thomas and his friends turned to see an engine racing toward them. It was Diesel.

"Nice stack, but I bet I could go higher," he bragged. He backed up to the car Thomas had been using and attached himself to it.

"Load me up, Carly," Diesel said.

"Hey, I'm not done yet!" Thomas protested.
The two engines tugged the car back and
forth. The tall stack wobbled and swayed,
then fell.

Just then, Gordon sped toward them.

Gordon was going too fast! He wasn't able to stop in time. His coupling broke, and he derailed, leaving his long train of cars behind.

"How am I supposed to make my delivery now?" Gordon asked.

Gordon's cars were filled with tires and bicycles, furniture and train parts.

"These items are old, but still useful," Gordon said. "I was on my way to Whiff's recycling plant."

"I can take them," Thomas offered. "I Thomas Promise!"

"It's too much for a little engine," Gordon said. There were six cars, all full.

A thought flew into Thomas' funnel. "I can take half and Diesel can take half," he said.

"That's a smokin' idea," Diesel said, letting black smoke drift out of his vents.

"We can race to see who gets there first," Thomas said. He wanted to prove he was still the number one engine.

Thomas and Diesel each coupled to three of Gordon's cars and took off toward Whiff's.

Both engines chugged along as fast as they could.

As they struggled up a steep hill side by side, Diesel saw a chance to make the race easier for himself. He tilted toward Thomas, causing a heavy refrigerator to fall into one of Thomas' cars!

Thomas tried to keep going up the hill,
but the extra weight made it harder. As
Diesel inched ahead, Thomas could feel the
heavy cars pulling him backward.
Suddenly, Thomas heard a *SNAP!*

Thomas watched, horrified, as his cars rolled back down the hill toward a dead end. He tried to chase them, but all three cars flew off the tracks—and so did Thomas.

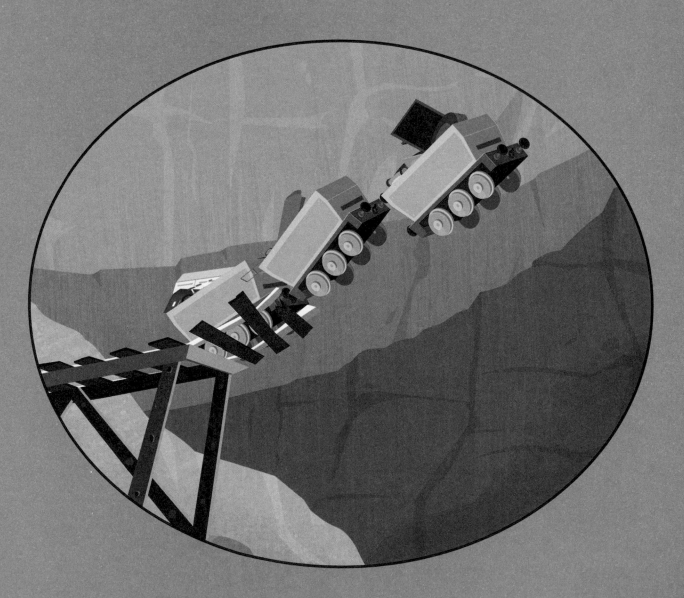

Thomas and his cars landed in a mud puddle. Percy, Sandy, and Carly raced after him to help. As Carly attached her crane to Thomas and started to lift him out, Thomas could hear Diesel tooting in the distance.

"I'm never going to win the race now," Thomas said sadly.

"But you promised Gordon you'd make this delivery," Percy said.

Thomas knew his friend was right. He'd made a Thomas Promise, and he wanted to keep it. He let Carly place him back on the tracks and started heading toward Whiff's.

As Thomas was making up time, Diesel was standing still. He was waiting for a drawbridge to come down so he could finish the race. He didn't want to waste his lead.

The moment the bridge was in place, Diesel lurched forward so suddenly that all his cars rattled and creaked. As he sped away, he didn't notice that his rear doors had opened. One by one, items tumbled out.

Thomas had almost caught up to Diesel when he noticed the cargo littering the tracks ahead.

"Diesel!" he called out. "Your cargo!" But Diesel couldn't hear him. He was speeding away, faster and faster.

Thomas stopped and picked up the fallen items.

Percy, Carly, and Sandy soon caught up.
"Why did you stop?" Carly asked.
"I still have a promise to keep!" Thomas explained.
"That means getting all of Gordon's cargo to Whiff's."

"We're going to help," Percy said. Everyone started moving the cargo into Thomas' cars. Before Thomas knew it, the job was done.

Diesel arrived at Whiff's and thought he had won, but Thomas and his friends arrived with all the cargo in tow.

"Thank you, Thomas, for keeping your promise," Gordon said.

"I couldn't have done it without Percy, Carly, Sandy . . . and Diesel," Thomas said. Diesel's cargo might have fallen out, but he had gotten it most of the way there.

Gordon was happy that his cargo arrived, but he still had a broken coupling. He didn't know how he would get his cars back to the station. "Maybe I can help!" Sandy said. She reached into one of Thomas' cars and pulled out an old hunk of metal. It was a coupling!

Gordon tried it, and sure enough, his cars coupled up
and he was ready to roll again.

"I guess these old things are still useful!" Thomas peeped.
Everyone smiled.

Diesel turned to Thomas. "Race you back?"
Thomas' smile got bigger. "You're on!"